D0044930

The Canine Crisis

by Steve Korté
illustrated by Mike Kunkel

Superman created by Jerry Siegel and Joe Shuster
by special arrangement with the Jerry Siegel family

PICTURE WINDOW BOOKS
a capstone imprint

Published by Picture Window Books, an imprint of Capstone.
1710 Roe Crest Drive
North Mankato, Minnesota 56003
capstonepub.com

Library of Congress Cataloging-in-Publication Data
Names: Korté, Steven, author. | Kunkel, Mike, 1969– illustrator.
Title: The canine crisis / by Steve Korté ; illustrated by Mike Kunkel.
Description: North Mankato, Minnesota : Picture Window Books, [2022] | Series: The amazing adventures of the DC super-pets | "Superman created by Jerry Siegel and Joe Shuster by special arrangement with the Jerry Siegel family." | Audience: Ages 5–7. | Audience: Grades K–1. | Summary: When the Cat Crime Club use kryptonite to capture Krypto the Super-Dog along with other members of the Space Canine Patrol Agents and steal money meant for Metropolis' animal shelter, Krypto and his pals have to figure out a way to escape and capture the wicked cats.
Identifiers: LCCN 2021054296 (print) | LCCN 2021054297 (ebook) | ISBN 9781666344400 (hardcover) | ISBN 9781666344448 (paperback) | ISBN 9781666344455 (pdf)
Subjects: LCSH: Krypto, the Superdog (Fictitious character)—Juvenile fiction. | Superheroes—Juvenile fiction. | Supervillains—Juvenile fiction. | Dogs—Juvenile fiction. | Cats—Juvenile fiction. | Theft—Juvenile fiction. | CYAC: Superheroes—Fiction. | Supervillains—Fiction. | Dogs—Fiction. | Cats—Fiction. | Stealing—Fiction. | LCGFT: Picture books.
Classification: LCC PZ7.K8385 Can 2022 (print) | LCC PZ7.K8385 (ebook) | DDC [E]—dc23
LC record available at https://lccn.loc.gov/2021054296
LC ebook record available at https://lccn.loc.gov/2021054297

Designed by Kay Fraser
Design Elements by Shutterstock/SilverCircle

Printed and bound in the USA. 4882

TABLE OF CONTENTS

They are a team of canine crime fighters.

They are a powerful pack of pooches.

They are led by Krypto the Super-Dog.

These are . . .

THE AMAZING ADVENTURES OF

the Space Canine Patrol Agents

Pups on Parade

It's a great day in Metropolis! The mayor announces that the Space Canine Patrol Agents (S.C.P.A.) are putting on a parade. The event will raise money for the city's animal shelter.

As the parade starts, Superman flies ahead to await the S.C.P.A.'s arrival at the animal shelter. Meanwhile, the canine crime fighters march through the street and display their talents.

Tusky Husky shows off his huge tooth. Hot Dog breathes fire. Chameleon Collie changes into a giant rabbit. Tail Terrier twirls his long tail like a lasso. And Mammoth Mutt doubles in size.

Krypto the Super-Dog flies to the head of the parade. He carries a giant bag. The people of Metropolis cheer from their windows and rooftops. They throw money into Krypto's bag.

Meanwhile, four evil members of the Cat Crime Club (C.C.C.) are standing on the ledge of a building. Their names are Purring Pete, Scratchy Tom, Gat Cat, and Kid Kitty.

With wicked grins, the cats toss glowing, green coins into Krypto's bag.

"Those coins are made of Kryptonite," snarls Purring Pete. "It is the one material that can harm Krypto!"

As Krypto catches the coins, he starts to feel dizzy. Then he falls.

The Super-Dog crashes to the ground.

Suddenly, Krypto hears calls of "Help! Help!" from the other members of the S.C.P.A. He sees them fall to the ground in a cloud of sleeping gas, but he is too weak to move.

Soon, the evil cats arrive to steal the money.

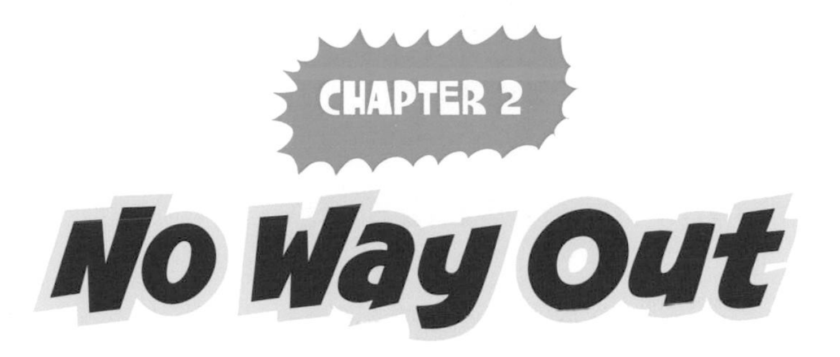

CHAPTER 2
No Way Out

A short time later, the members of the C.C.C. toss the helpless Super-Dog into a room with thick stone walls. The evil cats then zoom away in their plane.

The other members of the S.C.P.A. are inside the room with Krypto. When they wake up, the Super-Dog staggers to his feet and tries to break through the thick stone wall.

BUMP!

Krypto's head bounces off the wall.

"I don't know what's wrong," says Krypto. "The Kryptonite coins are gone, but I still don't have my powers!"

"Those feline felons are getting away with the animal shelter money," says Hot Dog. "We need to get out of here!"

"I have an idea," says Krypto. "First, we need to turn Tusky Husky upside down so that his big tooth is pointing into the ground."

"Tail Terrier, wrap your long tail around Tusky Husky," says Krypto. "The rest of you pull on Tail Terrier as hard as you can."

The dogs follow Krypto's instructions.

Tusky Husky spins like a top. His tooth drills a large hole into the floor.

The dogs escape through the hole. Chameleon Collie gives the weakened Super-Dog a ride on his back.

CHAPTER 3

Catching the Cats

After they escape, Mammoth Mutt looks closely at Krypto's collar.

"I think something green is glowing on the back of your S-Shield," she says.

Just then, Krypto realizes why he still feels weak. The C.C.C. must have put a piece of Kryptonite behind the collar around his neck!

Tusky Husky uses his sharp tooth to shatter the dangerous collar.

With his strength back, Krypto flies into action. He quickly catches up to the C.C.C. airplane. The Super-Dog grabs the plane and pulls it back to Metropolis.

Krypto bites a big hole in the side of the airplane. Then he clamps his paws on the plane and shakes it.

The cats and the bag of money come tumbling out of the plane and fall into the arms of the S.C.P.A. The dogs tie up the angry cats.

The canine crime fighters bring the bag of money into the shelter, where Superman is waiting.

"Nice job," says the Man of Steel. "You saved the day and raised a lot of money for the shelter!"

Superman ties Krypto's cape around the canine's neck. "When we get home I'm going to give you a brand-new collar," he says.

"Woof!" Krypto replies as he happily wags his tail.

AUTHOR!

Steve Korté is the author of many books for children and young adults. He worked for many years at DC Comics, where he edited more than 600 books about Superman, Batman, Wonder Woman, and the other heroes and villains in the DC Universe. He lives in New York City with his husband, Bill, and their super-cat, Duke.

ILLUSTRATOR!

Mike Kunkel wanted to be a cartoonist ever since he was a little kid. He has worked on numerous projects in animation and books, including many years spent drawing cartoon stories about creatures and super heroes such as the Smurfs and Shazam. He has won the Annie Award for Best Character Design in an Animated Television Production and is the creator of the two-time Eisner Award-winning comic book series Herobear and the Kid. Mike lives in southern California, and he spends most of his extra time drawing cartoons filled with puns, trying to learn new magic tricks, and playing games with his family.

"Word Power"

agent (AY-juhnt)—a person who acts on behalf of another person or group

canine (KAY-nyn)—a dog

collar (KOL-ur)—a thin band of material worn around the neck of a dog or cat

feline (FEE-line)—any animal of the cat family

felon (FELL-uhn)—a criminal convicted of severe crimes

lasso (LASS-oh)—a rope formed into a loop

mayor (MAY-ur)—the leader of a city

patrol (puh-TROHL)—to protect and watch an area

shelter (SHEL-tur)—a place that takes care of lost or stray animals

talent (TAL-uhnt)—something that you can do well and are good at

WRITING PROMPTS

1. Who is your favorite member of the Space Canine Patrol Agents? Write a paragraph explaining why.

2. Create your own Cat Crime Club member. Write down your villain cat's name and superpower. Then draw a picture of it.

3. At the end of the story, Krypto and his friends capture the evil cats. Write a new chapter that describes what happens to the villains or how they escape. You decide!

DISCUSSION QUESTIONS

1. Krypto is the leader of the Space Canine Patrol Agents. What makes him a good leader?

2. Krypto combines the talents of Tusky Husky and Tail Terrier to escape the locked room. What other powers or talents could the canine heroes have used to escape?

3. Which Super-Pet is the most powerful in this story? Explain your answer.

THE AMAZING ADVENTURES OF THE

Collect them all!